UNDER THE ARABIAN SUN

JANA HOPS TO THE TOP

Step boldly little one...

Written by Jean Wishart (Blackman) and illustrated by Mark Clemens

Preface

My inspiration for this story is born out of love. Love for my (then) newly-born granddaughter, and for the greater natural environment in which I live. I find myself constantly validating our region and proclaiming it a natural wonder.

This Desert is remarkable. It is nature at its extreme. That plants and animals have adapted and prospered as species in this vast and climatically harsh region is an ongoing source of enlightenment to me. It is a wonder that I wish to share. Its magic includes fine characteristics that touch on boldness, adaptation, respect and resourcefulness. It is these qualities, and others, that I wish to communicate to young readers. # Yes, it is possible to survive in a hostile environment.

To this end, I have created Jana, an extraordinary desert hare. Jana is the elder daughter of a family of hares living in the Arabian Desert, close to the outskirts of a tiny farming town.

I have been fascinated by desert hares since first observing them in the *Arabian Wild Life Centre* (Sharjah), and *Al Ain Safari Park* (Al Ain, U.A.E.). Should you wish to read more about desert hares and their companionable qualities, please see my website:

www.jeanblackman.com

- *Jean Wishart Blackman*

This story is for you, Jasmine.

Love you to bits.

Editing: Stephen Garrard

Agnes M. Holly

Illustrations: Mark Clemens

Thanks

To my cherished family - husband Roy, daughter Joanne, son Stephen, daughter-in-law Yuki and granddaughter Jasmine. Thank you for encouraging me to write this story. You could have laughed the idea right out of the water! You didn't. Your support will always be greatly valued.

Special thanks to Mark for taking on the mammoth task of illustrating this book. Ashleigh Blackman, my sweet artist (and stepdaughter), thanks so much for the very first paintings.

Ashleigh Blackman

When she woke up, the sun shining on her face, Mother Hare opened her golden eyes and stretched out, right from her fine hare toenails to the pointy tips of her ears.

"My golly gosh!" she exclaimed, clunking her head on a piece of rock. "Look at that blazing blue sky! It is late!"

Smoking sausages! It was hot. The bone-boiling heat hammered down on the massive desert sands. Small wild grasses and juicy shrubs were already flopping downwards seemingly looking for their shadows.

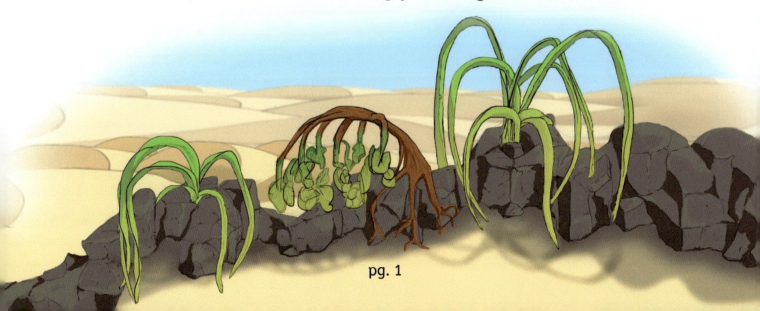

Mother, Father and their two young-hares lived in the Arabian Desert, just outside a tiny farming town. The town grew different crops; like dates, marrows and eggplants.

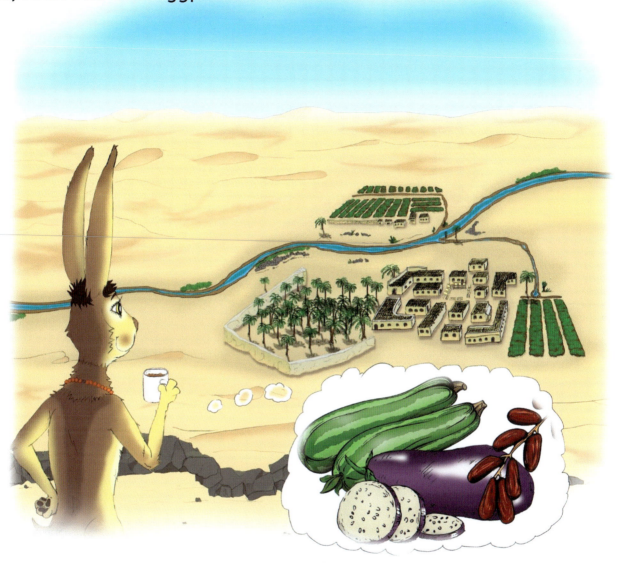

The Hare family lived beside some bulky desert rocks. Their home was a restful shelter, and very comfortable for little hares. Sure, the Hare family had their problems. Life was tough in the desert and trouble trampled all over the place. Father Hare firmly believed life in the desert was a test of strength and courage.

The Hares' lived on the land. Not in burrows. Their rock was huge and rather odd-shaped, giving them some shade during the day.

Jana was the elder of the two young hares. Her brother, Adam, was born a whole 5 minutes later. Slow to start, and slow to finish: Adam was a dawdler.

Mother, now wide awake, saw that Jana and Adam were still stuck in sleep. She poked them gently, hoping to wake them. It was not working.

Mother gave up, and decided it was time to make a noise! Mother shouted out, her voice cracking. "Breakfast Time!"

Instantly rubbing their groggy eyes, the two young hares wiggled their crumpled ears, and flexed their long skinny legs. "Breakfast? Breakfast was nearly always tasty!"

Jana sprang up at once and zoomed to breakfast. "Yummy! Marrow soup," she said, and tucked into the steaming sweet-smelling soup.

As Jana slurped her soup, Mother surprised her with a mouth-watering announcement: "I'm going to bake a cake today. Unfortunately, I do not have any eggs. I need eggs to bake a cake, a truly tasty cake."

Jana was all ears (which is not difficult for a desert hare!). "How many eggs do you need?" she asked, deciding at once that she was going to find the eggs!

"I'll need two eggs" replied Mother Hare, taken aback by Jana's eager interest in eggs. Jana appeared to be as pumped as popcorn. "Cake! I love cake," she sang out happily (sounding almost like a bird!). "I'll find the eggs!"

"Aha!" mused Mother, "so it's clearly the cake that is exciting Jana!"

Jana turned towards Mother. "Don't worry Mother. I will think of an eggs-cellent plan to find two fresh eggs."

Eggs...? *A good thinking place* was what she needed. Jana darted out to the shade of the nearby Ghaf tree. The leafy Ghaf tree flung cool shadows dancing freely onto the sand.

"Eggs, oh where to get eggs?" Jana let out a noisy whistle, almost tasting the sweet moist carrot cake in her mind. "Yummy" she simply must find the eggs!

"I see you have an issue there!" squeaked a voice from way up the Ghaf tree. "May I help you? I know just the place! And it's not even far. Hana, the hen has eggs. She is very grumpy today; perhaps you should wait until she calms down."

Startled, Jana looked up into the tree trying to spot the source of this information. The voice continued. "Hana is especially mad right now. Her feathers are ruffled. Someone is scaring her chicks." "Who is that speaking…?" asked Jana. Who are you?"

"It is I, the woozy bat of the Ghaf", said the voice. "My name is Babar, but everyone calls me Bat or Batty! I spend most of my life hanging upside down in this Ghaf tree.

Life looks different this way",

he chuckled, "and I like it!"

"There is a great deal that bats can do, you know. Our hearing is amazing – can you hear a feather fall? We can. And, our sharp eyesight, well we can see in the dark! Need I say more?"

"So, with my superb hearing, and my teeny sharp eyes, I get to know what's up in the world! Or is that down? Hmmm..."

Jana had stopped listening. She was thinking about the hen. It was crystal clear to her: Hana was in need of a friend. She needed help to protect her chicks.

Besides, Jana was not afraid of a snappy hen. Sometimes Mother Hare was snappy too, and she was a bold little hare. She knew exactly what she had to do, and that was to go and help Hana Hen.

"Bat, where's Hana's hen-house? I need to find my way there quickly."

"Clear-cut," replied Bat. "Hop over towards the town. You'll spot a largish signpost pointing the way."

"Blow me down!" said Bat, "a daring and caring young hare. Hop off our

wee hare and be careful, things are not always as they seem."

"Why the warning?" wondered Jana. "She pushed the thought to the back

of her head. Perhaps it came from all the hanging upside down!"

Jana waved goodbye to Bat. He barely stirred. He gave a lazy nod before dropping back to sleep. "I'll be off right away," declared Jana, hippity-hopping on her strong hind legs.

She was in a hurry! "I must help the anxious protective hen and her frightened chicks. Someone is troubling them!"

It was Jana's first outing into the desert all alone. She felt so grown up, and strong and brave, but also a little fearful.

Hana's hen-house was still some distance away, so she forced herself ahead in giant leaps and bounds.

Jana raced over the burning hot sand, thinking what a lucky-duck she was to have soft tufts of fur between her toe pads. Fine furry protection from the heat, so no sand could burn her! As she hurried across the scorching hot sand, Jana had an alarming thought.

"Crikey! Desert foxes!" The thought hit home. "I hope the chicks are safely inside the hen-house!"

Jana had heard that desert foxes

often munched on chicks.

After a while, the hen-house loomed straight ahead: all was still.

There were no chicks to be seen.

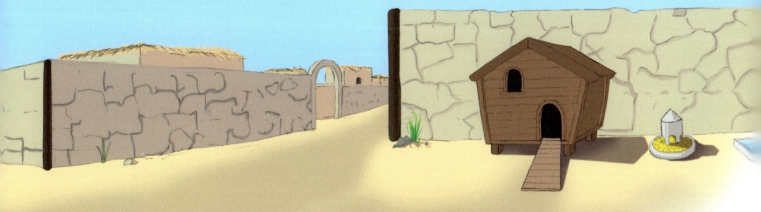

The silence shattered. Hana Hen burst out of the hen-house. She jumped, squawked and made awful rasping noises. She was very loud. Jana's heart raced like an F1 car.

"Don't worry Hana. I'm here to back you up," said Jana. "First things first -tell me why you are so flustered."

"Some rotten scoundrel is scaring my chicks!" snapped Hana. Her feathers were fluffed out making her look twice her size.

Hana was in a fowl mood, even more so than usual.

Jana began scouring the sands for evidence. Pretty soon she found some big, and unhurried looking tracks. "Look here!" she called to Hana.

"I spy pawprints outside the hen-house! They're great big deep ones!

"Oh no! Giant prints must surely mean bad news!" fretted Hana.

"Do not fear, Hana! I will make a plan.

Let me think…" replied Jana, wondering what to do or not to do.

Jana thought of her Father's hunting fables, those great stories about

chasing bad animals by following their hoof or pawprints.

"Aha! The mean beast must have left marks in the sand!" cried Jana. "I'll

follow them."

Jana tippy-pawed around the hen-house and just as she had predicted,

found more pawprints leading the way to some low-lying shrubs.

At first, Jana was undecided:

"Should I move into the shrubs

right away? Or should I set a trap?

What kind of beast could this be?"

Jana realised that she had no idea what kind of animal lay in store for her. Wisely, she decided to hide and wait until the big brute made the first move.

She crouched behind a nearby rock and signalled Hana to remain dead quiet. Jana was ready, her long ears tuned in for the slightest sound of movement.

Before long, Jana heard a

swish in the shrubs.

She watched intently, her

ears and eyes on red alert.

She felt a nervous,

bone-chilling tingle,

run down her body. "Who was rustling the shrubs?" Ooh, she was feeling

uneasy! First Jana spotted a pair of ears   - long black tufty ones -

behind shrubs.

They were not

foxy ears!

These were spikey spear-like ears, tips as black as the darkest desert

night. Then, Jana noticed the fur, reddish-brown in colour and then the

eyes, emerald

green eyes,

a colour she had

never seen before.

"Should she warn Hana first? Or call for help? Jana gathered both thoughts and did what hares do well in tricky situations... she let out an ear-splitting scream, sounding much like a hysterical striped hyena. The screech tore through the desert, right across plains and dunes.

The furry head behind the desert scrub was spooked on hearing the dreadful noise and suddenly, a whole mass of reddish-brown fur leapt out from behind the bushes. A wild cat, frightfully large and savage looking leapt out!

Jana thumped her legs loudly and rapidly on the sand, summoning help. There was no time for slow! Not content with this noise, she began mashing her teeth together too. The mashing and thumping made a deafening noise. It was hare-raising!

The cat gaped at Jana in surprise. "What an uproar from a rabbit!" he exclaimed, really astounded.

"Hare," corrected Jana, "I am an Arabian Hare and I have shouted out for help. Stop scaring the chicks, wild cat!"

"I am a Caracal cat", smirked the cat, "and I will not harm them. I like to

gawp and stare and ogle. I don't even

like the taste of chicken", he added. The

cat shifted on his feet and continued,

"I prefer to eat flying birds,

they're nice, wild and juicy.

The chicks, oh my day! I just watch the chicks

play, it's as simple as that. You should see them dance, sing, and jump

about. It's such

fun to watch!"

The cat paused to take a breath, then continued. "Why would I hunt them?

I can leap into the air and knock down at least ten flying birds at a time!

Chicks! Ha, too

boring for me,

thank you."

"But Cat, can't you see? The chicks are jumping and squawking from fear? They are not playing!" Jana rolled her eyes in exasperation. She looked at Cat and noticed something that bothered her.

"What is that red stuff dripping from your chin? It looks like blood." Jana felt confused and a little bit edgy.

"A snack", replied Cat. "I found it in the shrubs a moment ago, and it sure was tasty!"

"Really?" questioned Jana. "A snack lying in the desert shrubs? That is strange!"

Jana forced the words past her lips. "So, you're not going to eat Hana, the chicks or me?" she fixed her gaze on the Cat's eyes. The emerald eyes glistened and moved slightly sideways. Eventually, Cat answered.

"Nope".

"Well then, it's time we let Hana Hen know she needn't worry about her chicks. Poor Hana is one big jumble of nerves and fluffy feathers!"

The cat nodded. "Okay, I'm ready to calm things down." Jana looked closely at the cat, and decided to trust him.

"Well then," said Jana. "I'll call Hana and you, Cat, can explain everything to her, and apologize for alarming her chicks".

"What?" gasped the cat. "I cannot apologize! It's rule number three in the Cat Book of Rules, clearly stated in fact, that cats never ever apologize!" he added firmly.

Jana sighed, wondering how she will cope with a stubborn cat and an angry hen.

After some clear thinking, Jana hatched a fix-it plan. "Okay, I will do it," she offered, "I'll explain your Cat Rules and bizarre behaviour to Hana. I am sure she will be glad to hear her chicks are not in danger."

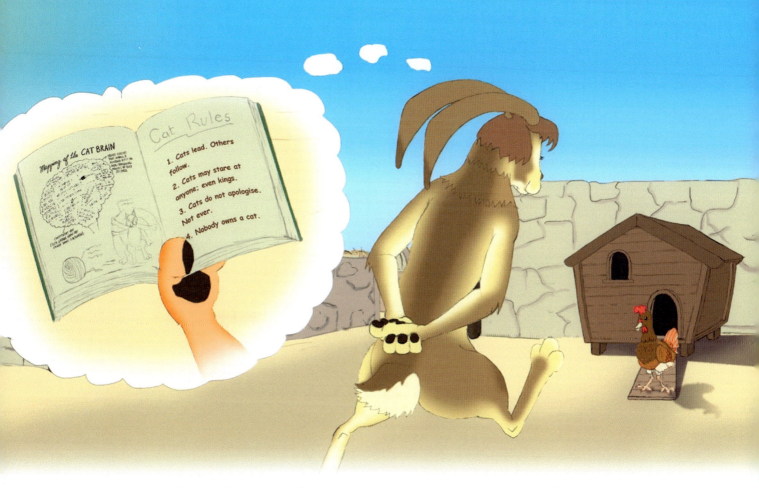

As Jana approached the hen-house, Hana stepped outside looking wary. "Who is it?" she asked.

Jana explained that the pawprints

belonged to a curious cat, who swore

that he would not harm the chicks.

He could not, however, apologize

because of Cat Rule number 3.

Jana then told her about the 'never- apologize' rule.

"I believe your chicks will be safe

outside now", added Jana, "but we

must watch Cat carefully, just in case."

Hana paused as she thought about it. "Right-ho. I feared a ferocious

feisty creature, not an inquisitive cat. A cat, well I can deal with that!"

She tilted her red-brown head, a beady eye on Jana, and asked, "What brought you to my hen-house in the first place, Jana?"

Jana explained the reason for her hurried trip to the hen-house, what Bat had told her, and how she wanted to help. "But, actually," she admitted, "all I was hoping for in the beginning, was two eggs for a cake!"

"Oh, my knobbly knee!" cackled Hana. "I have plenty of eggs and will be pleased to gift some to you!"

"Thank you." replied Jana. "Two eggs will be perfect for the cake, any more will be a wicked waste."

"Chicks!" cried Hana loudly, "Come outside to play! Be wary of the cat as he is not yet a friend," she warned.

Hana scuttled off to collect the eggs while Jana watched the young

chicks clowning and carrying on, generally having a jolly good time!

Eagerly waiting for the eggs, Jana happened to look up at the sky, and

saw that the sun was steadily sinking. The day was melting away, and

the early black of night was slowly creeping in.

Time to go home! She hopped about from one foot to another, hoping

Hana would come back soon.

Just then, Hana returned carrying two

beautiful smooth speckled eggs,

proudly packed into a gift box.

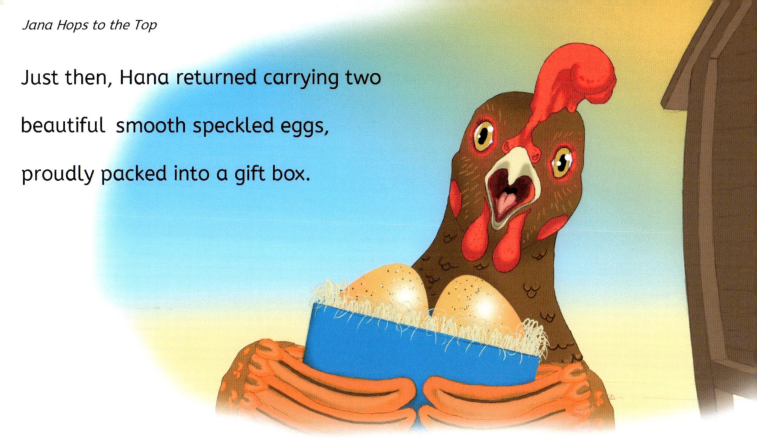

"Thank you for the fine eggs, Hana", said Jana. "My mother will bake a

delicious cake with them!"

"You're welcome, Jana!" Hana flapped her wing, scuttling away saying,

"now I must count my chicks to check them all in."

"Goodbye Hana" replied Jana as she readied herself to charge home. As

she set off, she heard a "meow" from behind some scraggly grass. "That

cat!"

"Good bye", purred the cat, "it's been quite nice to meet you, Jana."

Pondering whether the words "*quite* nice" were friendly ones, Jana decided that Cat was still a stranger. She turned to look back at him one last time. He had licked his chin clean. Jana noticed his tail flick, followed by a long stretching of his paw. She focused on his cruel-looking curvy claws, and as she did so, Cat bellied ever so slightly forwards.

Jana's gut jumped into action commanding her to "run!".

Without further delay Jana leapt up, taking giant hops with her powerful legs to speed home. Jana stopped only once, very briefly, to nibble on some super juicy wild scrub that happened to be there.

Back at the hen-house, Hana was busy counting her tired chicks. "9…10?

I'm a silly hen because each time I count the chicks, the number is

different!" I know that I have 10!

Frazzled and happy the chicks had fallen asleep, busily dreaming little

chicken-hero dreams.

While Jana was on her way home, Mother Hare was cooking up a feast.

Calling Adam, she asked, "Do you know when Jana will be home? Father

will soon be here, and supper is almost ready." Adam shook his head.

"Well then Adam, use this time

to clean your paws and comb

your hair," instructed Mother.

She giggled as she always did when she spoke about hair. "Why?"

Bang on time, Father Hare arrived home.

"Hello you two!" he greeted,

looking around as he did so.

"Where is our Jana?"

Mother Hare explained that Jana had gone out to look for eggs. As she was speaking, Adam heard a scraping of paws, followed by a shouted, "I'm home! I have eggs!"

"Well done Jana," cried Mother, "where did you find those lovely eggs?"

"It is a long story," replied Jana, "may I tell it after supper?" Jana was hungry!

"Well," answered Mother Hare "waste not, want not…let's eat supper. It's health-giving hare food!

The family gathered together to eat, agreeing that even the vegetables were paw-licking good.

After supper, Mother Hare turned to Jana. "Jana, please tell us about these lovely fresh eggs. Who did you get them from?"

"Well," began Jana, "it is a tale about a bat, a hen, and a cat."

"This sounds so interesting!" remarked Father. Mother and Adam nodded in agreement.

Jana told them all about her day in the desert, about Babar the bat and his dippy sayings; Hana the hen and her jittery chicks, and finally about the curious cat with the long, black-tufted ears and the blood-red chin.

"What an amazing adventure!" exclaimed Mother Hare. "You showed guts-gritting gumption out there!" Father Hare agreed enthusiastically.

Turning to Jana he said, "And I'm so proud of you for being a good friend to Hana." Then the tone of his voice changed, his face became all stern and serious, as he warned: "The desert is huge and new to you Jana, so be cautious."

Mother jumped up. "It is time to bake the cake! Why don't you all move away from the rocks, to the sands where the air is crispy cool?" she suggested, knowing that the moon's light was particularly brilliant.

Doing as she was told, Jana looked across at Bat's Ghaf tree. She thought of Bat's sayings: "full of beans at night, and sound asleep by day." She figured Bat was flitting about finding food.

When Mother's voice tinkled out calling: "Cake is ready!" Father and

Adam left swiftly, but Jana lingered, half hoping to see

her friend Bat again. From somewhere a murmured

whisper floated to Jana: "*A good deed is*

never wasted."

Mystified, Jana was left wondering about the words...who spoke them? A

witch? A wizard? A camel's mouth?

Still puzzling, Jana scampered home to be with Mother, Father and

Adam, and of course, to eat cake.

Happily plopping down until their tummies were full to bursting, the

Hare family chomped on the cake. They shared desert stories, and jolly

jokes (mostly about rabbits!)

All too soon,

it was sleep-time

for young Jana

and Adam.

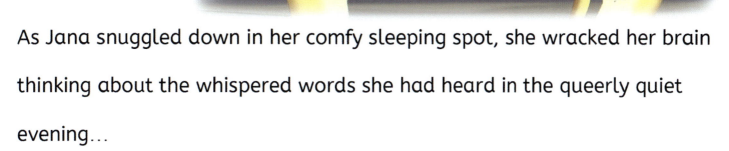

As Jana snuggled down in her comfy sleeping spot, she wracked her brain

thinking about the whispered words she had heard in the queerly quiet

evening...

"The soft voice?" she wondered. She thought of telling Adam that she had heard the skies whisper words. Words that had left her feeling so warm and cushy that she fancied she could jump over the moon with gladness. "No," she told herself, Adam wouldn't understand that.

Jana slowly stretched out, mulling over her busy dizzy day. She thought of Bat, Hana and the chicks, …the cat. She had met so many new faces – all in one day.

Flicking through her thoughts, she sensed a scratchy nagging feeling about Cat…was it his red chin? Red from a snack? Or was it his sticking-out curling claws?

"Cat snack…snack cat."

"Chick trick…trick chick."

"Good deed indeed."

The words tumbled inside her head, and she knew that something had been left undone… What the wizzes was it? Had Hana counted her chicks?

Too tired to think, Jana's weary eyes slowly closed. "Bat!" The bright idea

shot Jana's eyes wide open as she remembered that Bat would know the

source of the soft whispers, and

the mystery of

A good deed is never wasted

the mind-bending cat. Bat knew an awful lot! Anyway, nothing was

going to change, not during the night.

Sinking into her bed again, Jana looked up to the endless inky sky. The

moon's silvery beam, radiant

against the dark, grabbed her

attention. Jana watched,

spellbound, as moving pictures

began passing across the beam.

Pictures of Hana and her chicks,

asleep, and cuddled closely. Jana counted. Ten chicks, all safe and sound.

Next in the moon-glow were pictures of Cat, head bent, nibbling bitty berry-like cone shapes. (From a Juniper tree?) Cat lazily lifted his head, and Jana saw that his chin was red. Stained red from berry juice! One emerald green eye blinked at her, and the moving pictures ended.

Jana felt comforted, knowing all was well in the world.

"The desert is my home!" sighed Jana quietly, "and I love it."

The velvety soft fingers of Sleep kissed Jana's brow tenderly. She slid into a deep sleep, and dreamt incredibly splendid and magical dreams.

Jana grabbed hold of the dreams, locking them tightly against her little hare heart. As she slept, wondrous things were happening.

Stardust, from high in the sky, was sprinkling Kindness, right back to Jana, the brave little hare who dared and cared.

BEHIND THE NAME

Contextual Meaning

Jana   product of paradise/ rich harvest

Hana   bliss, felicity

Babar   highly powerful and influential, charming

Adam   a Prophet's name. Many have this name.

To read more about Jana, desert hares and the Arabian desert, visit the author's website:

www.jeanblackman.com

The desert supports life and where there's life, there's a story to be told…

watch this website for a sequel!